THE ZINGY ZAPPER

Peter Bently
Duncan Beedie

QEB

Hello! This is a story about four friendly monsters who live on Planet Pok.

This is **San**.

This is **Nid**.

This is **Gop**.

This is **Pem Pem**.

They have a funny way of talking. It's called Monsters' Nonsense.

See if you can read what they are saying. Ready?

Nid, San, and Pem Pem were on their way to have dinner with Gop. She wanted to show them her new invention.

After a delicious dinner of blue broccoli pie, Gop took out her invention. It made things magnetic.

Nid wanted to try the Zingy Zapper first.

Nid had given himself a mega dose of ZAP!

Foff!

Suddenly all the knives, forks, and spoons flew off the table.

Then, Gop's cans of pickled blue broccoli burst out of the kitchen cupboard. Followed by...

...Pem Pem's roller skates!

Bock bock!

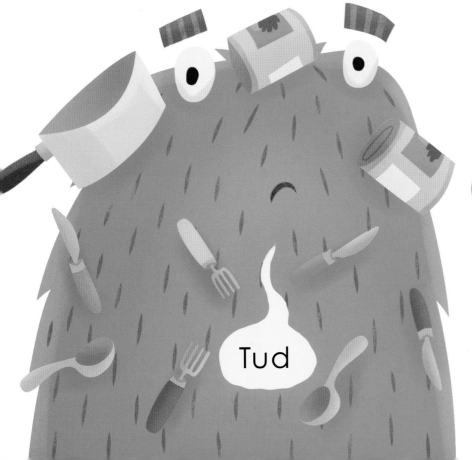

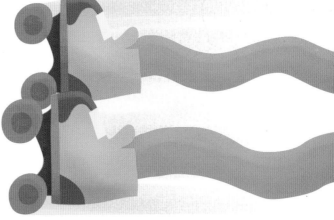

They came flying through the air and so did Pem Pem!

Gop grabbed the Zingy Zapper
and switched it from ZAP to ZING.
She pointed it at Nid.

Lell tam
mit toff!

Nid stopped being magnetic and all the
metal things dropped to the ground.

San wanted to try the Zingy Zapper next. She switched it to ZAP. But she tripped on Pem Pem's skates.

Guck neb lod!

Everyone laughed as the ZAP shot far into space.

When the monsters had finished tidying up, it was nighttime. Muddy Moon and Metal Moon would soon appear.

The monsters whizzed off to Muddy Moon in Gop's spaceship.

Gop asked if the Mudlings had seen Metal Moon.

Fuff feff

Huck?

Metal Moon had flown off toward Planet Pag.

The monsters said a quick thank you and escaped to the spaceship. What naughty Mudlings!

Gop zoomed away and steered for Planet Pag. As they got closer, they saw Planet Pag's Violet Volcano looming up before them.

Gop's spaceship started hurtling toward it. Gop slammed on the brakes, but they kept going faster and faster!

BUMP! They crashed. Gop went outside to try to fix the spaceship. But her Space Spanner flew out of her grasp! It was stuck to the volcano.

The volcano was a giant magnet. San must have zapped it when she fired the Zingy Zapper.

Oll foll!

Gop quickly gave the volcano a blast of ZING!

It worked.
The spaceship
broke away from
the volcano and
hovered in the air.

Hupsot

The Space Spanner flew
back to Gop and she
caught it in one hand.

Suddenly, they heard a loud rumbling noise from inside the volcano.

It sounded like it was about to erupt! They flew off in the spaceship, just as the whole volcano shook and...

As Metal Moon zoomed back home, the monsters got ready to leave. They were on their way back to Planet Pok when they saw...

...a Mudling! It had sneaked on board. Next stop— Muddy Moon.

Reading with your monsters!

Monsters' Nonsense is all about having fun while learning the skills of reading. If children have fun reading, they'll want to do it more.

What helps children with their reading?

Phonics: the ability to sound out (decode) words that they don't know.

Reading comprehension: to read for meaning so that they can understand and enjoy the story.

The *Monsters' Nonsense* series is designed to support these skills to help children become successful, happy readers and to encourage a positive, shared reading experience.

The adult reader (or reading mentor) reads the main narrative—supporting reading comprehension and bringing the story alive.

The child reads the Monsters' Nonsense in the speech bubbles. These are "non-words" to help them practice their decoding skills at a level that is right for them. It's important that your child knows that these "non-words" are not real words and have no meaning.

More monster fun

Monster Questions Ask your child questions about the story. For example, which monster invented the Zingy Zapper? What does it do? Who lives on Muddy Moon? Why did the spaceship crash? What was stuck in the Violet Volcano? Why? What do they think would happen if they took a Zingy Zapper to school?

Monster Spells Give your child a whiteboard or paper and a pen. Tell them you are going to say some of the non-words (in a silly monster voice) and ask your child to write them down. Remind them to think of how many phonemes (sounds) there are in each non-word and match them to the correct graphemes (letters).

Monster Story Encourage your child to draw or make some more monsters for Planet Pok. Think of some new names and see if your child can spell them. Ask your child to think of a story for their monsters. You can help write the main narrative and your child can write the non-words.

Phoneme Count Ask your child to throw a beanbag or ball into a basket/bucket for each phoneme they hear in a given word. For example, d/e/p (3), f/u/ff (3), l/a/ff/m/o/d (6), s/e/b/l/i/t (6). Ask your child to say the sounds they hear as they throw each beanbag. When they are done, ask them to count the number of beanbags to determine the total number of phonemes for each word.

Phonics glossary

blend to blend individual sounds together to pronounce a word, e.g. s-n-a-p blended together reads snap.

digraph two letters representing one sound, e.g. sh, ch, th, ph.

grapheme a letter or a group of letters representing one sound, e.g. t, b, sh, ch, igh, ough (as in "though").

High Frequency Words (HFW) are words that appear most often in printed materials. They may not be decodable using phonics (or too advanced) but they are useful to learn separately by sight to develop fluency in reading.

phoneme a single identifiable sound, e.g. the letter "t" represents just one sound and the letters "sh" represent just one sound.

segment to split up a word into its individual phonemes in order to spell it, e.g. the word "cat" has three phonemes: /c/, /a/, /t/.

vowel digraph two vowels which, together make one sound, e.g. ai, oo, ow.

Encourage your child to use monster voices. This can be lots of fun!

Quarto is the authority on a wide range of topics.

Quarto educates, entertains and enriches the lives of our readers—enthusiasts and lovers of hands-on living.

www.quartoknows.com

Publisher: Maxime Boucknooghe
Editorial Director: Victoria Garrard
Art Director: Miranda Snow
Editor: Sophie Hallam
Designer: Mike Henson
Consultant: Carolyn Clarke

Copyright © QEB Publishing, Inc 2016

First published in the United States in 2016 by QEB Publishing, Inc.
Part of The Quarto Group
6 Orchard
Lake Forest, CA 92630

A CIP record for this book is available from the Library of Congress.

ISBN 978 1 60992 912 1

Printed in China